DRACULA vs. GRAMPA

AT THE MONSTER TRUCK SPECTACULAR

WILEY & GRAMPA'S CREATURE FEATURES

DRACULA vs. GRAMPA

AT THE MONSTER TRUCK SPECTACULAR

WRITTEN AND
ILLUSTRATED BY

KIRK SCROGGS

LB
1837

LITTLE, BROWN AND COMPANY

New York ⚓ Boston

This book is for Harold & Betty & Diane & Corey
And is in memory of Guy Scroggs
and Charles Scroggs, master monster drawer and cool dad.

Special thanks—

Suppasak Viboonlarp, Mark Mayes, Kris Gee, Simeon Wilkens,
Jackie Greed, Rosa Jimenez, Amy Pennington, Inge Govaerts, Michael Moss

Andrea, Sangeeta, Saho and the Little, Brown crew—woo hoo!

And special super-duper deep-fried thanks with ranch seasoning to
Ashley & Carolyn Grayson and Dan Hooker

Copyright © 2006 by Kirk Scroggs

Little, Brown and Company

Hachette Book Group USA
237 Park Avenue, New York, NY 10017
Visit our Web site at www.lb-kids.com

First Edition: July 2006

Library of Congress Cataloging-in-Publication Data

Scroggs, Kirk.
   Dracula vs. Grampa at the Monster Truck Spectacular/written and illustrated by Kirk
Scroggs.—1st ed.
   p. cm.—(Wiley & Grampa's creature features; #1)
   Summary: When Grampa and Wiley sneak out of the house on a stormy Halloween night
to attend Colonel Dracula's Monster Truck Spectacular, they run into trouble from which
only Gramma and an F5 tornado can save them.
   ISBN 978-0-316-05902-2 (hc) / 978-0-316-05941-1(pb)
   [1. Grandparents—Fiction. 2. Vampires—Fiction. 3. Halloween—Fiction. 4. Humorous
stories.] I. Title.

RZ7.S436726Dra2006
[Fic]—dc22

2005044436

10 9 8 7 6 5 4 3

CW

Printed in the United States of America

Book design by Saho Fujii

The illustrations for this book were done in Staedtler ink on Canson Marker paper,
then digitized with Adobe Photoshop for color and shade.
The text was set in Humana Sans Light and the display type was handlettered.

CHAPTERS

CHAPTER 1

It Takes Guts!

Ladies and gentlemen, boys, girls, dogs, and upper marsupials . . . the story I'm about to tell you is so frightening that I can't recommend it to the faint of heart, pregnant mothers, children under 46" tall, or the easily spooked. If you're scared of bats, rats, or old hippies, then this tale is definitely not for you.

So turn the page if you think you've got the guts. Otherwise, **BEWARE**! Children, grab your mammas! Elderly, take your heart medication! Prepare yourselves for the ultimate in raw terror. . . .

Don't get scared yet! That's not a monster. It's just Grampa. And that goop in his hand? Those aren't the brains of some poor kid. . . .

2

Those are pumpkin guts. You see, it was
Halloween night and Grampa was having his
annual jack-o'-lantern carving contest. That's
me, Wiley, next to Grampa and over there,
that's Merle the cat torturing a june bug.

"WILEY, MY BOY!" said Grampa, pausing to put on a record. "The secret to an expertly carved pumpkin is to set the proper atmosphere. For tonight's listening pleasure I have selected "The Sound of Mucus" followed by "Old MacDonald Had One Arm and Ninety-nine Buckets of Blood on the Wall."

"Two of my favorites!" I replied.

4

Alas, it was my turn to gut the next victim.

"YUCK!" I grimaced as the stringy orange goop squished between my fingers.

"Kinda looks like one of your Gramma's casseroles, huh?" Grampa joked.

"I HEARD THAT!" yelled Gramma from the kitchen. "There'll be no Halloween snack treats for you if you keep that up!"

Gramma's casseroles may taste like pumpkin innards, but her Halloween snack treats are *par excellence* (that's French for "pretty darn good"). My favorite is her Screaming Skull popcorn balls with marshmallow brains inside.

At the awards ceremony, my one-eyed pirate was a hit, and Merle the cat presented a simple yet effective piece. Of course, we were no match for Grampa, whose carving of a Mediterranean village clutched first prize — not surprising since he was also the only judge!

"I call it *Pompeii Before the Eruption*," bragged Grampa.

"Show off," I muttered.

CHAPTER 2

Just Kickin' It

Next on the agenda was some serious rest and relaxation. Grampa and I kicked back, turned on the tube, and snacked on some black cherry soda and Pork Cracklins (that's deep-fried pig skin in layman's terms).

"OLD MAN!" yelled Gramma from the kitchen. "You better not get any pork crumbs on my new chair!"

"SHHHHHH!" I shushed. *"The All-Night Mega Monster Scare-a-thon* is about to begin!"

Dracula Down Under, The Nebraska Weed Whacker Nightmare, and *Mayonnaise: The Motion Picture!* So turn out the lights, pop some corn, and prepare for utter terror! Tonight's flicks are brought to you by Velvet Knuckles hand lotion. For smooth skin that smells like honeysuckle, it's gotta be Velvet Knuckles."

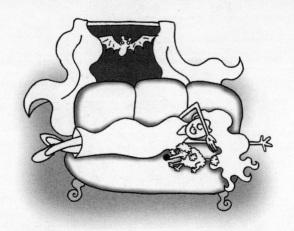

The Dracula flick started off with a bang.
A beautiful girl was sprawled on a sofa as a
fanged creature of the night approached. He
hovered above her, ready to chomp, and then . . .

some guy who's had too many chili dogs comes on chuggin' a bottle of Pepty Bizmo.

"It never fails," complained Grampa. "Just when it's getting good they gotta cut to a Pepty Bizmo commercial! It's just disgust—"

CHAPTER 3

A Dream Come True

That's when it happened! A TV commercial so awesome it stopped Grampa in mid-gripe.

"Tonight only!" shouted a crazed announcer. "The Gingham County Colosseum presents **Colonel Dracula's Monster Truck Spectacular**! Witness over 200 monster vehicles, including the world's only vampire truck! With special musical guest eight-year-old country sensation Lil' Buckaroo and the Texaflo Supreme Unleaded Dancers! Tickets are still available!"

We stared at the TV, trembling.
Pork bits fell from our mouths.

"World's only vampire truck,"
I said.

"Texaflo
Supreme Unleaded
Dancers,"
Grampa drooled.

"Meow,"
meowed Merle.

But our bliss was
short-lived.

CHAPTER 4

Shattered Dreams

Channel 5's smarmy weatherman interrupted, "Hi, folks! Blue Norther here! I hate to ruin any trick-or-treat plans, but Channel 5's Whopper Doppler Radar has picked up an F5 tornado in the vicinity and if you've seen *Twister*, you know that's a big one! So stay indoors, stay tuned to me, don't do anything fun whatsoever, and have a wonderful evening!"

"Grampa," I pleaded, "we've just gotta get to that truck show! I don't care if there is an F5 tornado!"

"Wiley," Grampa replied, "there are more dangerous things than an F5 tornado."

"Like what?"

"Like your Gramma if she finds out we're going to a monster truck show in the middle of an F5 tornado!"

But it was too late. Gramma stepped in saying, "Don't you two get any harebrained ideas about going to that truck show! Didn't you hear Blue Norther? There's foul weather afoot!"

Now, Gramma's known to have a temper. You see that thing on her head? That's her anger meter, and the needle in Gramma's anger meter was starting to move into the red zone — a zone you *don't* wanna visit!

GRAMMA'S ANGER METER

Grampa was torn. Sure, the idea of ridiculously souped-up monster vehicles destroying one another was hard to resist.

But was it worth risking certain death by tornado and flood?

Or, even worse, the wrath of Gramma?

I was sure Grampa would make the right and responsible decision.

So he lied to Gramma and told her we were
going outside to check on the hounds.
"BE BACK IN TWO HOURS!" Grampa yelled back.
Gramma looked pretty, pretty miffed.

Outside, the wind was picking up and thunder rumbled. The storm was approaching! Grampa's two hounds, Esther and Chavez, were already well prepared.

CHAPTER 5

The Trek

On our trek to the colosseum, we saw Nate Farkle trick-or-treating with his kids.

"Storm's coming!" he warned Grampa. "Blue Norther says there could be an F5 tornado, and if you've seen *Twister*, you know that's a big one!"

"I've napped through F5 tornadoes!" Grampa bragged.

Grampa has been known to exaggerate, but I can verify that he *did* nap through the Great Septic Tank Explosion of 1999.

"Wiley," said Grampa, "if we wanna make it to the truck show in time, we're gonna have to cut through those woods."

"You mean those dark, scary, wild animal-infested woods?" I asked nervously.

"Why, that's the best kind, my boy!"

CHAPTER 6

The Woods

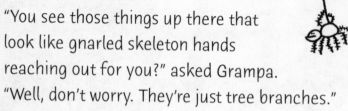

"You see those things up there that
look like gnarled skeleton hands
reaching out for you?" asked Grampa.
"Well, don't worry. They're just tree branches."

"And those slimy things moving down around
your feet? Don't worry. Those are probably just
snakes looking for someplace warm, like your
pants leg, to curl up for the night."

"Thanks for the words of comfort," I said.

"Don't look so worried, Wiley. Everything's
gonna be just fine!" said Grampa.

Boy, was he wrong.

Lightning flashed!

The wind wailed!

Golf ball–sized hail
pounded my head!

Grampa napped!

CHAPTER 7

The Gingham County Colosseum

Finally, we crawled out from the woods—muddy, wet, and itchy. There before us was the Gingham County Colosseum — at least, I think it was the Gingham County Colosseum. Something about it just didn't seem right.

MONSTER TRUCK SPECTACULAR

TICKETS

Inside, the place was a madhouse, stuffed to the brim with freaky people.

"Grampa," I said, "all these fans look pretty weird."

"It's Halloween, Wiley!" said Grampa. "Everyone's wearing costumes . . . or just really ugly."

Colonel Dracula stepped out in a black suede cape and plaid shirt and greeted the crowd in a funny accent.

"Velcome to the show, my vonderful friends! Tonight you vill see the most terrifying trucks ever to prowl the streets of Gingham County! But first, let me introduce our opening act!"

That's when Drac, accompanied by the Texaflo Supreme Unleaded Dancers, broke into a showstopping rendition of the disco classic "I Vill Survive."

"I think Drac should just stick to monster trucks," complained Grampa.

Finally, Drac brought out the vehicles. "This is gonna be good!" declared Grampa as the trucks hit the floor.

There was the **Behemoth Broncosaurus**!

Vlad, the Impala!

The **Invisible Van**, though it wasn't much to look at.

Even a **Werewolf Winnebago**!

"And now, ladies and gentlemen, I present my finest creation," said Dracula. "The **Mudsucker**! The vorld's first and only vampire truck!

"Ten liter, eighteen cylinders, all-veel drive, moon-roof, twenty-five disc CD changer with detachable front, and six cup holders! And best of all — it drives itself! It took twelve mad scientists and twenty-three hunchback assistants over a century to create this baby!"

"Now," continued Drac, "I'll need two volunteers from the audience to help demonstrate the awesome appetite of the Mudsucker!"

"You hear that, Wiley?" said Grampa. "Raise your hand, quick!"

"I am, I am," I said, frantically waving my hand, **"BUT THIS ISN'T FAIR! THAT KID'S GOT SIX ARMS!"**

But to our shock and delight, Dracula chose us!

"You, the delicious-looking young child and that leathery, bony old creature beside you. Come on down!"

"Who's he calling old?" complained Grampa.

The crowd cheered for us as we stepped out into the arena.

CHAPTER 8

Skip the Lobster

"And now, these brave fools vill get into this classic **British Mini Pip-squeak** and play the ultimate game of chicken vith my monster truck! The Mudsucker and our guests vill take off at opposite ends of the arena, jump these ramps, and collide head-on above this fiery pit of giant mechanical lobsters!"

"**BOY!**" said Grampa. "And to think we were just going to stay home and watch TV all night!"

"WAIT A MINUTE!" I shouted. "This sounds like suicide!"

"Nonsense, my dear boy," said Dracula quietly. "I guarantee it is all perfectly safe. This is all just an act. There is no danger vat — so — ever. Now, if you vould just sign these insurance papers and an organ donor policy before ve begin."

We suited up, got in the Mini Pip-squeak, and waited. The tension was unbearable, as was Grampa's underarm odor.

"Sorry," said Grampa, "jumping over flaming pits of robot shellfish makes me perspire!"

Suddenly, Drac gave
the signal.

The Mudsucker took
off like a surface-to-air
missile launched from
the molten core of an erupting volcano!

Grampa took off with all the fury of a
riding lawn mower with three wheels and a
broken muffler!

The Mudsucker reached the end of the ramp and launched into the air like a mighty metal bird!

Grampa drove over the edge, straight into the open claw of lobster numero uno!

"WELL, THIS IS IT, WILEY!" said Grampa.
"Snuffed out by a giant crustacean! I guess
this is payback for all those seafood platters
I've enjoyed over the years! If I'd only ordered
the steak!"

But, lucky for us, the Mudsucker swooped in and clamped the lobster's claw with one of those lobster-clampy things. We heard a loud **CRACK!** and the lobster released our car from its deadly grip.

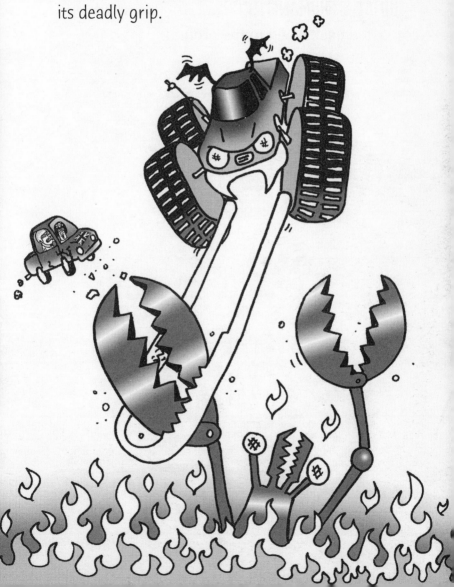

Then the Mudsucker caught us in its truck bed and, just for good measure, flung the metal lobster into a giant pot of boiling water.

"WHAT SHOWMANSHIP!" said Grampa as we coasted back down to the ground.

The crowd stood up and cheered as we exited the Mini Pip-squeak. I was never so glad to be back on solid ground.

"LET'S GIVE IT UP FOR OUR BRAVE VOLUNTEERS! VOO VOO VOO!" Drac yelled, pumping his fist into the air. "You see, I told you it vas completely safe."

"I knew it all along, Drac," said Grampa, trembling. "Now, if you don't mind, I'll be needing a heart specialist and a fresh pair of drawers!"

After the lobster incident, it was time for the halftime show with Lil' Buckaroo performing his country smash "Can I Get a Yeehaw?"

Grampa and I decided we'd rather chew on rusty barbed wire than listen to Lil' Buckaroo, so we headed for the snack bar.

CHAPTER 9

The Quest for Snacks

We waited in line at the snack bar while a rather shaggy gentleman purchased a big, hairy tarantula burger.

"I don't know much about truck show cuisine," I confessed, "but I've never seen tarantula burgers on a menu."

"It's not so strange, Wiley," said Grampa. "I ate a caterpillar cheese dog at the boat show just last April!"

Suddenly, I got the feeling that someone or something was looming over us.

Sure enough, Colonel Dracula was right behind us . . .

and he was staring at Grampa's wallet, mesmerized by the photo of Gramma standing in front of Grampa's 1956 Buick!

"Are you enjoying the show, my courageous lobster tamers?" Dracula asked.

"We sure are, Drac!" replied Grampa. "We braved rain, hail, and an angry Gramma just to see your tour de force of vehicular carnage!"

"Then perhaps you and the boy vould like a backstage tour vere you can meet the Mudsucker up close and personal?" Dracula offered.

"YOU BET VE VOULD!" exclaimed Grampa.

I wasn't so enthusiastic.

CHAPTER 10

Drac's Lair

WATCH YOUR HEAD LOW CEILING

Dracula took us deep into his cavernous lair.

"Please excuse the mess," he pleaded.
"The maid vas eaten by a rabid porcupine."

FRAGILE!

YE OLD MONSTER CART SHOW

CHRISTMAS ORNAMENTS

FRAGILE!

FRAGILE

XXX

XXX

Bats hovered above us. Spiders scurried below.

"VATCH YOUR STEP!" Dracula warned. "My piranha love the taste of small children."

"I HOPE YOU BROUGHT YOUR SWIM SUITS!"

Drac said as we passed a rather uninviting swimming pool.

"No thanks, Drac," said Grampa, politely, "I always wait one hour after eating a tarantula burger before swimming or belly dancing!"

Drac's lair was most impressive. He had his own haunted library . . . a well-stocked, rat-infested wine cellar . . .

and even a plasma TV!

MARTHA DRACULA
1820-1895

Past Drac's entertainment center and hanging above his hot tub was a strangely familiar portrait.

"LOOK, GRAMPA!" I shouted. "That picture looks just like Gramma!"

"Aaaah, yes," Drac said. "She vas my beautiful bride. She is no longer vith us. Dead for over vone hundred years! I'd rather not speak of her right now."

Drac got a little mushy and, I must admit, I got a little choked up myself. Tears were shed. Noses were blown. It was pretty disgusting.

All of a sudden, the lights went out!

"Grampa," I whined, **"I DON'T LIKE THIS!"**

"Don't worry, Wiley," replied Grampa. "There's gotta be a reasonable explanation for the power outage. Could be the storm, maybe Drac didn't pay his electric bill, or maybe a thousand angry rats have gnawed through the wiring and are heading toward us right now. It could be anything."

It was then that the lights came on again and Dracula was right behind us with the Mudsucker!

"BOY!" said Grampa. "This night is putting my pacemaker to the test!"

"Please," said Drac, "come closer and inspect my greatest invention! Don't be frightened. She von't bite!"

"She's a beauty, Drac! Let's pop the hood and see what this sucker's made of," Grampa said as he climbed onto the truck and peered into the engine. "Hey, Drac! Where is the carburetor in this baby?"

"It's underneath the tongue," Dracula said.

"OH YEAH!" Grampa replied. "There it is."

CHAPTER 11

Looking for Trouble

While Grampa drooled all over Drac's truck, I
decided to do what all smart kids
do in scary stories — go
exploring by myself in the dark.

Drac's lair was bigger than I had ever imagined.
I saw enormous parlors, ballrooms, and
spooky crypts.

He even had escalators, pay phones, and fast-food joints. This place was impressive! In fact, I wasn't scared at all . . .

until, of course, I found Drac's collection of
petrified skulls.

Then, to make matters worse, I backed right into Drac's assortment of non-friendly reptiles!

I quickly decided it was time to get back to the truck and find Grampa!

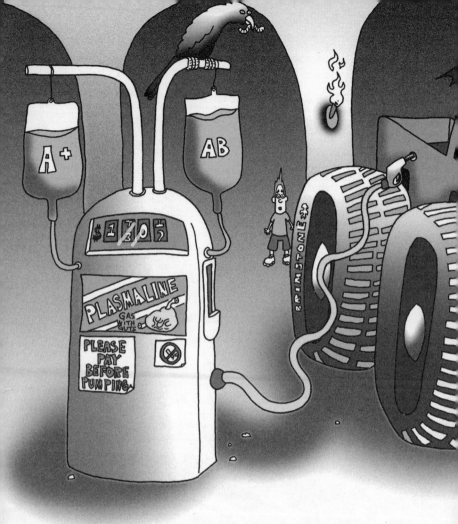

That's when I noticed that the Mudsucker was being refueled, but not with gasoline. It was being filled with, with . . . well, let's just say it's red and gushy and rhymes with **FLOOD!**

CHAPTER 12

Time to Go!

"OH MY, LOOK AT THE TIME!" I said, pushing Grampa toward the door. "We gotta be going!"

"Wiley," Grampa said angrily, "Drac was just about to show me his collection of ancient torture devices!"

"Trust me, Grampa," I said as we moved into the hallway, "we need to get as far away from this place as possible."

"Adios, Drac!" shouted Grampa. "We'll see you at the tractor pull next Thursday!"

As we made our way down the main hall, we heard a strange sound behind us. We stopped and turned to find the Mudsucker speeding toward us!

"Your Gramma never lets me drive the Buick in the house like that," complained Grampa.

"RUN!" I screamed.

And we ran . . .
through the corridors of the colosseum,
past the tarantula burger stand,
over Lil' Buckaroo . . .

We ran all the way to the exit, where
we found . . .

To our horror, there at the door was Gramma, and boy was she mad! Her anger meter was in the red, and we are talking redder than a sunburned lobster on a barn door!

"Well, Wiley, we made our beds and now we have to lie in 'em," said Grampa. "It's either the monster truck barreling toward us or the fiery anger of your Gramma. I'm seriously considering sticking with the truck."

But Grampa came to his senses and we quickly
got into Gramma's car.

"HURRY, GRAMMA!" I pleaded.

"DON'T YOU HURRY ME!" she snapped back.
"I'll teach you to lie to your . . ."

CHAPTER 13

Never Lie to Your Gramma!

Gramma's saucy tirade was cut short by the blinding headlights of the Mudsucker.

Dracula was right behind us!

"STEP ON IT, GRANNY!" yelled Grampa.

"CONSIDER IT STEPPED ON!" shrieked Gramma.

"MEOW!" meowed Merle.

Gramma took off and hit warp speed in 6.5 seconds!

"WILEY!" Grampa yelped. "It's been nice knowing you! I only wish we could have lived to see that mayonnaise movie!"

CHAPTER 14

It's a Twister! It's a Twister!

Gramma sped through the hills like a madwoman.

And wouldn't you know it? Right in front of us, blocking the road, was an F5 tornado! Blue Norther was right!

"Hold on to your drawers!" Gramma yelled.
Then she did something that's ill-advised
(unless you're being chased by a vampire truck) —
she signaled and passed the twister on the left.
It worked, too! We lost the Mudsucker! I gave
Gramma and Merle the high five and Grampa . . .

Grampa was napping.

CHAPTER 15

Home Sweet . . . Uh-Oh!

At long last, we made it home. I shook Grampa awake.

"Eeeeyaaaa," he groggily yawned. "What'd I miss?"

"Just me saving your scrawny rear end from an F5 tornado," Gramma replied.

"Guess I napped through another one," he said as we pulled into the driveway to find . . .

Okay, now you should be scared. Dracula was waiting for us in the driveway with the Mudsucker at his side!

Grampa bravely jumped out and confronted
Dracula.

"ALL RIGHT, DRAC!" Grampa challenged. "What
do you want with my beloved family . . . and
Gramma?"

Drac, sensing danger, assumed the famous Trembling One-Footed Bat stance!

Grampa, ready for the mother of all showdowns, struck his Crouching Cobra stance.

Gramma stuck to the more traditional Rumbling Shifty-Foot technique . . .

and Merle coughed up a mean hair ball!

I had to do something, so I valiantly jumped in.

"I know what you're up to, Drac! I saw how you
looked at that photo of Gramma in Grampa's
wallet, and I also got a good look at that portrait
in your lair, which looks just like Gramma.
Not to mention that you've been pumping that
vampire truck with some pretty disgusting bodily
fluids! It all points to one obvious conclusion!"

"It can't be too obvious," Grampa complained.
"I'm terribly confused."

CHAPTER 16

Wiley's Theory

So I unveiled my theory: "Drac is after Gramma! She looks just like his long-dead wife. He wants to make Gramma his new vampire bride for all eternity!"

"OH MY!" said Gramma.

Wiley's Theory Debunked

Dracula laughed, "No, no, no, my dear silly boy! Your Gramma is a lovely voman and she does resemble my dear dead vife, but it vas the **CAR** that I vas admiring in the photograph! I vant that 1956 Buick! I used to have vone just like it back in the day. Ahhhh, those vere the good old days. Riding around town, drinking black cherry soda vith my baby."

I must admit I felt a little bit foolish, but I was also extremely relieved.

Drac got a little teary eyed, and Grampa gave him a hug.

Even Merle and the Mudsucker made friends.
Everyone was happy. . . .

Except Gramma. She was a
little disappointed.

CHAPTER 18

The Shady Transaction

Grampa happily sold Drac the Buick and even threw in a bag of Pork Cracklins.

"Drac, I gotta be honest," said Grampa, "this car breaks down about every other week and the weeks in between."

"It matters not," said Dracula. " I shall give it a complete tune-up and lube job, and then I vill replace the engine with the heart of a Siberian volf hound!"

"Hey, whatever works," said Grampa.

Drac got so overjoyed with his new car that . . .

He turned into a bat!

"You people are so kind," Drac said, "and to think I vas considering draining the blood from your necks and feeding it to my truck."

"OH, YOU CHARMER!" Gramma said, blushing.

"**COME, MUDSUCKER!**" summoned Dracula.
"You must return me to the colosseum before
dawn!"

And they took off into the night.

"WHEW!" Grampa exclaimed. "Thank goodness!
Storm's over! Sold the car! No harm done. . . ."

CHAPTER 19

The Wrath of Gramma

A strange silence fell over us. Gramma was angry. In fact, Gramma's anger meter had moved from red to a new color never before seen by human eyes!

"What kind of grampa," she started, "drags his grandson through the woods in the middle of a tornado to see a truck show run by bloodsucking vampires?"

"But Gramma," I argued, "what kind of grampa would be **COOL** enough to drag his grandson through the woods in the middle of a tornado to see a truck show run by bloodsucking vampires?"

"The boy's gotta good point," said Grampa.

So that's my story, folks! As you can see, despite our night of unrelenting terror, everything turned out okay!

Grampa and I got home in time to see the explosive finale of *Mayonnaise: The Motion Picture.*

Gramma needed a new car, so Drac gave us a good price on the Invisible Van.

And Drac even joined Grampa and his buddies for Friday night poker. (**Grampa's poker tip #235**: Always let the vampire win!)

And as for the Mudsucker . . .

Let's just say, thanks to a deal I worked out with Drac, I had the coolest show-and-tell **ever**!

CRACKPOT SNAPSHOT

Gramma needs your super sleuthing skills to point out the differences between these two photos before she puts 'em in her wallet and shows them to her friends at the beauty parlor!

The answers are on the next page. No cheating!